Savage

Hellish #12

Charity Parkerson

Copyright

—Warning: This book is intended for readers over the age of 18.

Introduction

A human meets a fox shifter. There are a lot of

lies in that sentence.

Pip is obsessed with boxing. The bouncing and striking calls to his inner fox. When Celeste gives him a ringside ticket to the light heavyweight championship match, Pip is over the moon. Seeing his favorite boxer, Savage Holiday, up close is like a dream come true. Then Savage looks his way and Pip discovers what really drives his passion for the sport. Turns out, it has nothing to do with boxing at all.

Savage never notices anyone when he's in the zone. Adrenaline always keeps him focused on winning and nothing else. There's something about Pip's eyes, though. They're almost unnatural. Savage's attention is caught. He can't explain the draw, but

Savage can't stay away. Pip is odd and playful. He's nothing like the rough and tumble crowd Savage normally runs with. He makes Savage want to risk everything. It's a race to see which of their secrets ruins them first.

The Hellish Clan is back as—once again—Celeste has paired an unlikely couple. The delicate situation needs to be handled as tactfully as possible. Except Jonathan and Celeste are in charge. That means things are handled as dramatically as possible. Now, let's see if Savage can handle it.

Chapter One

THE CROWD WAS LOUD AS HELL against Pip's sensitive ears. There were a thousand reasons why Pip rarely left the safety of King Jonathan's land while in this plane. The inability to tolerate loud noises was a minuscule excuse. Humans smelled funny. Pip had to venture past his comfort zone tonight, though. He would never forgive himself if he missed this event. Fights this big rarely came to New Orleans. Most big-name boxing matches were reserved for places like Vegas. Tonight, in the rarest of opportunities, Pip's favorite boxer, Savage Holiday, had a match to retain the light heavyweight championship. It was the biggest moment of Pip's life.

Boxing was the only sport he followed. He had

fallen in love after catching one match on TV at the bar. Savage had been fighting that night too. As a fox, Pip had been immediately mesmerized by the way Savage bounced on the mat. Pip had wanted to hop too. That was the first sensation that captured his attention. Then the camera had focused solely on Savage. Pip's breath had stopped. Everything had gone still. He was beautiful in a rugged way— like a warrior. Pip had stood on his barstool to get a better look. He hadn't even realized he had done it until the bar's owner Raff had fussed at him. Pip had flashed Raff an apologetic smile, but then he had gone right back to staring. Savage was solid muscle and sad eyes. Dark hair and firm-looking lips. Pip wanted to see him smile. Tonight, he was some-where in this building. Pip just wanted to set eyes on him. That was all. Celeste had given him a ring-side ticket because she was the most amazing mom in all the worlds.

The announcers read the names, weights, titles, and accolades. Pip swung wildly between covering his ears from the noise and standing in his seat. His gaze locked on Savage's form as he made his way toward the ring. Everyone else disappeared. Outside the ring, Savage paused, doing his final checks with the officials. With a satin robe covering him and the hood hiding his face, Pip couldn't see him. He stared so hard, his eyes itched. Savage turned his face slightly. It was enough. Their gazes met. Pip didn't think it was all in his head. Savage didn't smile. His expression gave nothing away, but he also didn't break eye contact until someone said his name. The hair stood on the back of Pip's neck.

Pip's lungs deflated when Savage looked away. Wow. Savage was breathtaking. His eyes were green. Pip would never forget this night. That one moment had been enough to last him the rest of his life. Amazing.

BOUNCE. BOUNCE. BREATHE. Savage looked for his opening. Breathe. His opponent, Mitchell Brown, was well known for not having any tells. Still, Savage watched. He would find his opening. Savage had negotiated a deal where he could fight on his turf. He wouldn't lose his strap in his hometown. Mitchell dropped his shoulder. An evil chuckle rang through Savage's mind. He struck. Mitchell went down. Savage bounced on his toes, waiting. Watching. Mitchell didn't move. The count seemed slower than usual as time moved at a crawl. He fought the urge to look ringside. The bell rang. The ring official raised Savage's arm. Months of nonstop training for two minutes of fight time. The perfect scenario.

Savage's gaze couldn't be controlled any longer. It moved ringside. His stare found the same yellow eyes focused on him as they had been before the match. The tiny guy with strawberry-blond hair bounced in place, clapping. So he was there for Savage. Savage smirked. The hair stood on the back of his neck. He tried shaking off the spell those yellow eyes weaved. Savage couldn't look away. His trainer, Ace, stormed the ring. He jumped up and down, hugging Savage and lifting him off his feet—

the big bastard. Savage's gaze slid back toward yellow eyes. He was getting away.

Savage yelled in Ace's ear, "I need a favor." He forced Ace to look yellow eyes' way. "Do you see that guy in the blue Henley? That's my friend. Don't let him get carried away by the crowd."

Ace slapped Savage's back so hard, he knocked the air from Savage's lungs. "On it." Ace leapt from the ring and chased after Savage's prey. Savage's stomach muscles clenched. He had no idea why he had done such a thing. Savage told himself he would meet with a fan. That was something fighters did all the time. He would give some autographs. Learn the guy's name. There was nothing weird about this at all. He was driven by the high of his win. Nothing else. That didn't explain why Savage's gaze kept finding the tiny guy, latching on, and refusing to budge. This time, the guy was gone, and Ace jumped back into the ring as Savage answered reporters' questions.

Ace touched his lips to Savage's ear. "I told Pip to meet you in the parking lot out back in twenty minutes. That way, he doesn't get bombarded by your fans."

Savage nodded, trying to act like nothing was out of the ordinary. His muscles were so tense, he wondered if he would snap a tendon. The guy's name was Pip. Fucking adorable. Savage couldn't be done with this part fast enough.

IF PIP DIDN'T LOVE THE OUTDOORS, he might have given up and gone home. After Savage's trainer had chased him down, Pip had gotten a bit nervous. He wasn't the bravest person under the best of circumstances. Savage wanting Pip to wait for him wrecked his nerves until Pip found a way to entertain himself.

The parking lot where he had been directed to wait was dark and mostly empty. At the edge of the lot, yellow fixed concrete bollards lined the edge of the concrete, stopping cars from driving through the grass. Alone and with nothing else to do, Pip climbed on top and leapt from bollard to bollard, keeping himself entertained.

"Goddamn. You've got amazing balance."

Pip had smelled him coming. Savage had the most amazing scent Pip had ever encountered. Pip liked it way too much. Tempering his excitement, Pip turned Savage's way and dropped to the ground.

He landed lightly on his toes. His gaze never budged from holding Savage's stare. Pip couldn't explain it. It was like there was a current between them, linking them. "Hi. I didn't think you'd show."

"I didn't think you'd wait."

A smile exploded across Pip's face. "I guess we were both wrong." The way Savage stared at Pip made Pip's stomach quiver. He was incredibly intense. "You were amazing tonight. I knew you would win."

Savage's mouth lifted in one corner. "Would you like to go for a walk?"

Pip nodded. He still didn't understand why Savage had sought him out, but Pip liked the way his stomach felt in Savage's company. It was like when Celeste fed him his favorite foods and then rubbed his belly.

They fell into step beside each other and headed away from the arena. Side by side, they made their way toward the river. Block after block disappeared behind them before Savage spoke again.

"Is it weird that I don't even know why I asked you to wait for me?"

"I don't know," Pip answered honestly. "I'm glad you did, though. You feel nice."

Savage chuckled. It was a deep and rumbling sound that curled Pip's toes. "I don't know what that means."

Pip bounced a little as he fought to explain. Sometimes his thoughts weren't very linear. "It's like a sixth sense thing, I guess. You're quiet and soothing. Never mind. I guess I don't make sense."

They made it to the gazebo by the river. Savage

walked inside and sat. His gaze focused on Pip, making butterflies stir in Pip's stomach. "No. You don't make sense, but I still get you. I don't do this."

Pip's forehead furrowed in his confusion. "What? You don't walk?"

A sexy laugh burst from Savage. "No. I meant I don't have my trainer chase men down to meet with me. There's something about you. I don't know what it is. It's like you came to see me tonight."

"I did come to see you tonight." Even Pip heard the confusion in his voice.

Savage had an amazing smile. "You're adorable. I love that life obviously hasn't beaten the innocence from you yet. How old are you?"

Pip had to think about it. Immortals didn't age the same as humans.

Tell him twenty-one.

Pip nearly sighed in relief at Celeste's mental intrusion. He felt better, knowing she kept an eye on him.

"Twenty-one."

Savage blew out a sigh. "A babe in the woods."

Well, that was true in more ways than Savage would ever know. Pip decided to change the subject. "I was surprised to hear about tonight's fight being here in New Orleans. Isn't this usually a Vegas thing? Not that I'm complaining."

Savage sprawled out, spreading his knees, and leaning back to rest his elbows on the wood behind him. He was such a big guy. Pip wanted to snuggle down in his lap. "My manager negotiated a deal so I could have the hometown advantage. Mitchell didn't really have the stuff to fight me. So I made

16

him come to me."

Pip climbed onto the bench opposite of Savage. He walked along one of the boards, incapable of standing still. It was dark. The fox in him wanted to play. "Does that mean you live here?"

"Yeah. You didn't know that?"

Pip focused on Savage. "How would I know that?" Even Pip heard the confusion in his voice.

Another sexy rumble of laughter vibrated from Savage's throat. "I guess I sounded pretty conceited right then. Usually, when I meet new people, it seems like they know more about me than I do. I guess I assumed you had Googled me."

"Oh. No. I haven't done that." Pip wasn't one hundred percent sure what that was.

Savage shook his head. His smile didn't abate. It kept making Pip's stomach feel weird. "You're...

a little strange."

"Oh." Pip had nothing. Strange didn't sound good. He looked around. He could smell humans milling about in the shadows, but everyone kept to themselves. He didn't fit in this world. Tonight had been nice, but it seemed like it was time for him to move along. His most favorite boxer in the world had gone for a walk with him and found him weird. That was a blow. Pip forced a smile to his face. "I guess I should go. You probably have friends and whatnot." Unlike Pip.

My sweet foxy. You're not alone, baby. You have me.

Pip tried to feel less sad as Celeste's words brushed his mind. Celeste was who the humans called their God. Pip was her fur baby. He had no right to feel anything but blessed.

"Yeah. I suppose I should let you go be young."

Pip cocked his head to one side and studied Savage's face. "Are you not young?"

"I'm a thirty-year-old professional boxer. I'm fucking ancient."

"What do hu—people do when they're young?" Pip really needed to leave. He had almost said humans. Savage already thought he was strange.

Savage shrugged. "You know, the usual. Drink. Go to clubs. Take home strangers for a night of no-name mind-blowing sex."

Pip blushed. "That's definitely not me." Pip hopped down, landing lightly on the ground. "It was nice meeting you. Thank you for the walk."

Savage stared at him in silence, as if he didn't know what to make of Pip. After a moment, Savage shook his head. "It was nice meeting you too, Pip. Be careful on your way to whatever it is you do for fun."

Pip nodded. He reluctantly moved away, sliding into the shadows. It had been an unexpected and amazing night. Pip would likely talk Celeste to death when he got home. His excitement was off the charts. He had gotten one heck of a fan experience. Pip doubted anyone would believe it, but it was time to go home now. Pip didn't belong in the human world. As much as he loved his time with Savage, it was over.

SAVAGE STARED AT THE SPOT WHERE PIP disappeared. He felt strange—like he had let someone important get away. His feelings didn't make sense. He couldn't explain it. It was in his chest. He felt like he was drowning.

"Are you really planning to let such a sweet and obviously helpless thing like that walk alone through the dangerous streets of NOLA?"

Savage's head whipped around as a blonde bombshell slipped inside the gazebo from the opposite side. She almost glowed in the darkness and in her beauty. Even though she wasn't his type, Savage wasn't blind. It seemed like she should be the one scared of being alone. Still, she had a point. Pip did strike him as way too sweet, innocent, and helpless to be walking alone at night through these streets.

He glanced around. "Isn't it a bit dangerous for you to be alone?"

She chuckled. It was a musical sound that made

Savage's heart rate slow. He suddenly felt at peace. "Sweetie, I am the most dangerous thing on these streets. Now go get your man before he gets hurt."

Savage stood. Even though he still felt like he shouldn't leave her alone, Savage wanted to go after Pip. This chick was right. He needed to keep Pip safe. Savage couldn't explain why. Pip just felt like his responsibility. "Stay safe out there, all right."

Her eyes flashed with laughter. They seemed to capture the light in an unnatural way—like they were the light. She waved him away. "Get lost."

Savage didn't need to be told twice. He jogged after Pip. He spotted Pip's retreating form and called after him. "Hey, Pip. Wait up."

Pip turned his way. His eyes also seemed to flash unnaturally. Savage wondered if the moon was in some weird phase tonight, making everyone a little weird. Then Pip smiled and Savage forgot what he had been thinking about. "Hey."

"Let me walk you to your car. This town is dangerous."

"I don't have a car."

That one stumped Savage. "How are you getting home?"

Pip didn't answer right away, as if he thought it over. "A cab, I suppose."

Nope. He wasn't. Savage couldn't let the guy get ripped off by a cabbie. "I'll drive you home."

Again, Pip didn't answer right away. After a moment, he smiled. "Are you sure? I live kind of deep in the woods."

All the more reason Savage should drive him. "Good. That'll give me more time to get to know you."

With a little bounce in his step, Pip nodded and turned away. His smile and barely contained energy were infectious as hell. Savage couldn't explain anything that happened so far tonight, but he craved Pip's company. He made Savage feel young and light. Everyone else made Savage feel heavy with the weight of his title. He had to represent his brand every second of the day. Pip had come to see him tonight, but Pip didn't act like he cared that Savage was the light heavyweight champion. It was freeing. Savage wanted to know everything about the guy.

"What do you do for a living?"

Pip always took his time answering questions. Savage loved that he obviously thought before speaking, even when it came to mundane things. It didn't feel like anyone used their heads any longer.

"I'm a home companion."

That was sweet. Savage could feel the good-ness radiating from Pip. "That sounds fitting. You seem like you'd be good at that."

Pip flashed him a smile. "What do you do out-side of boxing? What else is close to your heart?"

Savage shrugged. He liked talking to Pip. "It's sad to admit, but nothing. The last few years, I've been training and dealing with sponsors. I haven't felt like I've done anything else. That's done for a while, though. I had already decided, after this fight—no matter the outcome—I would take some time off."

Pip kept glancing Savage's way, looking like he cared. It was nice. "What do you plan to do first with your new freedom?"

Savage led Pip to his truck before responding.

The lights flashed as he neared. He opened the passenger side door for Pip. After Pip climbed inside, Savage met his stare. "First, I plan to take you home. That way, I'll know where you live. Then I plan to show up tomorrow and take you to dinner."

Pip dipped his chin and blushed.

Savage shut the door before Pip could shoot him down. He honestly had no clue what had gotten into him tonight. Savage should have been questioning his sanity. At the moment, he didn't care about anything but spending more time with someone nice. Still, he half expected Pip to reject his dinner plans as he climbed behind the wheel. Savage had made a lot of assumptions tonight. It was only a matter of time before he stumbled onto a wrong one.

Pip didn't say a word beyond giving Savage an

address to type into his phone until they were ten minutes into their drive. "I never really thought about meeting you. If I had, I wouldn't have expected you to be this nice."

Savage quickly glanced Pip's way before going back to watching the road. He felt the need to clear away that misconception before Pip found himself disappointed. "I'm not nice in the least. Truth be told, I wouldn't be taking you home at all right now if I wasn't trying to learn where you live. I'm pretty fucking selfish when I want what I want."

Pip didn't respond.

Savage glanced his way again, dying to know Pip's thoughts. Pip was smiling. It was a sweet and secret smile—like he was happily surprised to learn Savage was interested in him.

"Mhmm. Damn." The pleased curse escaped

Savage without thought. He honestly couldn't recall being this drawn to anyone. The more time he spent in Pip's company, the more his hunger grew. His impatience made him greedy. It felt like it took forever to get to Pip's place. He came to an iron gate and slowed. "Hellish?" The letters spelling out that single word twisted the arch of the gateway, confusing Savage.

"It's a Scottish Clan. You can drop me off here, if you want. I can walk up the driveway."

Savage snorted. "I'll get you to the door." He navigated up the long driveway. The flash of animal eyes captured Savage's attention. "Did I just see a wolf?"

Pip made a humming sound. "They're domesticated."

"A Scottish clan with domesticated wolves.

Who exactly are you working as a companion for?" Savage asked as the massive mansion came into view. It was amazing. The place was too big to see the entire thing.

"Her name is Celeste. This is her grandson's home. It's a long line of old money."

Savage put his truck in park. "It looks like it." His gaze slid Pip's way. Savage immediately forgot their surroundings. "What time am I picking you up tomorrow?"

Pip visibly fought a smile. "Um, I guess whenever. I don't have anything else going on."

"Cool. I have an interview at two. I'll come get you after that and we can figure something out from there." On that note, he jumped from the truck and circled around to Pip's side. Savage didn't want to give Pip time to get away. He opened Pip's door and reached to help him out. As their hands met, a surge of electricity ran up Savage's arm. He couldn't let Pip go, even after Pip's feet were safely on the ground. The open door and the lifted vehicle combined with their dark surroundings gave the illusion of intimacy. Savage found himself shuffling closer. Pip didn't try to slip away. He was such a tiny guy. Savage had to lean down to go in for a kiss. He barely pecked Pip's lips before Pip's head jerked back—like Savage had surprised him. Savage snagged the back of Pip's neck and hauled him forward. He held tight, ensuring Pip couldn't get away this time. Savage nipped at Pip's lips until Pip opened for him. Between his big win and meeting Pip, a feeling of power surged through Savage. He hauled Pip even closer. Things turned hotter by the second. His body was on fire. Savage felt like he knew himself better in that moment than he ever had. As desperate as he was for Pip's body, Savage tried cooling things down. He had enjoyed Pip's company. Savage genuinely wanted to see Pip again. Maybe he wouldn't come back if Pip took him to bed now. He couldn't say. Before he could make the decision to end their kiss, Pip slipped beneath his arm and eased toward the front door. "Thank you for the ride. I'll see you tomorrow."

Savage blinked as Pip rushed inside, leaving Savage behind. A smile tugged at the corners of his mouth. Anyone else would have dragged Savage inside. Pip looked like he couldn't get away fast enough, and Savage didn't think for a second it was an act. Pip was shy and awkward. Sexy as fuck. Goddamn. That kiss had him hard enough to bend steel. A motion at the edge of his vision caught Savage's attention. A tiny fox hopped through the grass. Savage couldn't look away. He was mystified by the amount of wildlife he had seen since he had arrived. The fox stopped and stared. Savage shook his head. It had been a strange night. He couldn't wait to do it again.

Chapter Two

PIP'S HIND LEGS TWITCHED AS Celeste scratched his belly. He had been dozing for hours in her lap as she read. With a book in one hand and her head in the clouds, Celeste absently scratched and rubbed Pip's belly, filling his quota of attention for the day. He hadn't stopped thinking about Savage and that kiss. It had been an amazing slice out of time, but Savage was human. Pip still intended to see him again. He just couldn't get attached. Savage wouldn't likely spend hours sitting in place, giving Pip the attention he craved in fox form. In fact, Savage would likely come unglued if he ever learned the truth. Pip wasn't good at keeping secrets. He wasn't sure if there was any point in seeing Savage again. As much as Pip longed to be with him, he didn't know if anything good could possibly come from it. Only heartbreak would be found at the end of that road.

"I think it's time for me to send you to Jonathan," Celeste said, setting her book aside. "Your date is getting impatient to see you."

Pip skittered onto his paws. "*Do you mean he's already there?*"

"Yes, sweetie. You had best hurry. The boys are having a bit too much fun with him."

Even though Pip didn't know what that meant, he still felt a spurt of jealousy. Savage belonged to him. The boys couldn't have him. Pip balanced himself on Celeste's lap and licked her face. Her laughter made everything worthwhile. She was his goddess. His mommy. He loved her and his time with her in the heavens. As a descendant of the goddess Inari, Pip was one of the few creatures allowed to walk freely between the worlds. He was only a godling. Unlike Nephilims, he had been created rather than born. His powers were miniscule compared to Celeste's or Jonathan's. He was a much watered-down version of a god. Still, he could stay here with Celeste and that was a good thing.

Celeste held his face between her hands and placed loud kisses on his furry cheek. "Oh, sweet baby. I love you so much, but you deserve to have a life outside of me. Savage is waiting. He's rather sweaty and gorgeous right now. You don't want to miss that."

At the idea of a sweaty Savage, Pip leapt from Celeste's lap and into his bedroom at Jonathan's inside the mortal realm without looking back. As his feet touched the ground, Pip transformed into a man. With a snap of his fingers, he dressed. Being a godling might mute him, but he had some perks. He would use them now to get to Savage as quickly as possible. Now that he was here and emotions were no longer muffled by the heavens, his heart seemed to roar to life. His skin tingled with anticipation. Pip no longer felt satiated by belly rubs. He wanted to play with Savage.

Pip followed the scent of his human. The house felt empty, which was strange. Jonathan's home usually felt teeming with life. It was rare for the vampires to be outdoors during the day. While they could tolerate the sunlight, it zapped their powers. The guys usually lounged in bed during their weakest hours. He couldn't imagine what would be important enough to give up mate time to head outside.

As soon as Pip stepped into the backyard, he spotted Evan and Tam sitting together near their cauldron. Instead of working on potions, as usual, they sat side by side, watching the men huddled together in a group. Pip's eyes latched on to Savage in the center of it all. He wore the same outfit as the Scots: a kilt and nothing more. Celeste was right. He was rather sweaty and sexy as sin. Pip couldn't believe this man had kissed him last night. His stomach felt all jittery at the idea of it happening again. Pip liked him a lot.

Savage's head turned Pip's way. His gaze found Pip as if he felt Pip's presence. As Pip looked on, Savage's mouth lifted in one corner in a sexy smirk. Pip pressed his hand to his stomach. He forced himself to take a breath.

Tam called out to him, breaking the spell. "Hi, Pip. Come sit with us and watch the action."

Pip forced his feet to move Tam's way. He really wanted to kiss Savage, but he didn't feel like Savage's kisses belonged to him. Rather than follow his heart, Pip dropped to the ground at Tam's side.

"What did I miss?" He glanced Tam's and Evan's way. "And why is Evan in wolf form?"

Tam's blue eyes shone bright with good humor. Between that and his soft-looking blond hair, Tam always looked like a tiny angel. People gravitated toward him, even though Tam didn't feel comfortable around everyone. Today, Tam seemed a bit more sociable—like excitement had him opening up.

"Evan was a wolf when your man showed up. He's waiting for a good time to change without being conspicuous. Did you see that our men are in kilts?" Tam fanned his face.

Truthfully, Pip hadn't seen anyone other than

Savage. He dutifully eyed the men out of loyalty's sake. Sure enough, Tam's mate Riskel and Evan's mate Bleidd were in kilts too. Risk's dark skin gleamed with sweat while Bleidd's long silver hair was up in a bun. There was a lot of prime meat on display.

"I see that. I'm glad you saved a front-row seat for me."

Tam chuckled. "You've missed so much," Tam said, excitedly. "First, your man showed up and Faolan was like, 'Who the bloody hell are you?' and Savage was like, 'I'm here for Pip.' Well, from there, things kind of spiraled out of control. The guys kind of took turns threatening Savage's manhood and peppering him with questions. Savage said he was a boxer and I asked what a boxer is and Faolan said it was a fake fighter." Tam took a breath. "And that's the short version of how every-one ended up in kilts doing a mini version of the Highland games."

A shadow fell over Pip.

Tam kind of jumped and squeezed the poppet he carried with him everywhere to deal with the PTSD from years in Hell.

A sexy muscular arm reached past Tam to pet Evan. Pip followed its line until he stared into green eyes that stole his breath.

"Hey."

That was all the greeting Pip got before Savage claimed his mouth. Pip's soul let out a happy sigh.

"Awww, I love to watch new mates kiss. It's magical."

Tam's words fell like a ton of bricks. He was right. Celeste wouldn't put him in this situation for no reason. She had chosen him a mate. Fuck. He turned away from Savage's kiss. Tam was unabashedly staring. Evan was sprawled across Tam's lap. His gaze was every bit as locked on Pip and Savage. Neither of them looked a bit ashamed.

"Evan says not to stop on our account."

A sexy chuckle rumbled from Savage's throat and vibrated against Pip's skin as Savage kissed the shell of Pip's ear. "I got a little carried away with your friends."

Pip forced his mind to let go of its shock. "I was just getting the story from Tam. It sounds like a classic case of Faolan fever. He has a way of goading people into shenanigans. It's okay, though. You can borrow my shower later."

Savage feigned offense. "Are you saying I stink?"

"He's saying he wants you naked," Tam said, making heat explode through Pip's face.

Another sexy rumble of laughter fell from Savage's gorgeous lips. "Anytime he likes." On that note, Savage left Pip alone to pray for the earth to swallow him whole.

He shot Tam an accusing look.

Tam didn't seem the least bit ashamed. "Am I wrong?"

May the gods help him, Tam wasn't wrong at all. Things weren't that simple, though. Savage wasn't one of them. Pip didn't know how to feel about it. On one hand, Celeste was so amazing. She had handed Pip's biggest secret crush to him on a silver platter. On the other, he felt a little sick. Savage didn't want him because he wanted him. He was only attracted to Pip because Celeste made him that way. Nothing felt right.

Tam brushed his hand down Pip's arm, petting him. "Please don't. Mates are a blessing."

Pip tried for a smile. Sometimes he forgot how powerful Tam was. There wasn't a mind safe from him. With Pip sitting so close, Tam likely couldn't close his mind to Pip's thoughts.

Tam went back to stroking Evan's fur while keeping up his conversation with Pip. "Eventually, she had to pair you with someone. Keeping you tied to her solely as a pet forever would have been cruel. No matter who she picked, you'd feel the same. Just because you love her, that doesn't mean your pick is unfair. It's not like you asked for him. She's simply giving you a shot at winning him. Do you have a better shot at winning him than some other guy walking down the street because you're Celeste's fur baby? Maybe, but then again, maybe not. Personally, I think he still would've chosen you. I mean, look at him."

Pip glanced Savage's way at Tam's urging. Savage stared back at Pip with hunger in his eyes.

As the hunger grew in Pip's gut, Tam leaned closer to his ear. "You tell me, did Celeste only give you what you wanted? Or did you climb onto a barstool in the middle of Raff's to get a better look at the soulmate she had already chosen for you? Celeste rarely thinks about the now of anything. Her vision is a lifetime ahead of everyone currently living."

Damn. Tam was right. Something had drawn Pip to get closer to the TV the first time he had seen Savage fight. At the time, he thought he had been mesmerized by the movements. Now Pip realized he had spotted his soulmate. Pip had to explain to the poor guy that nothing in the world was as it seemed. Pip had no idea how he would pull that one off.

WHEN SAVAGE HAD SHOWN UP AT PIP'S place, the last thing he had expected was to be met by a band of kilted miscreants. Thankfully, Savage was always up for a challenge. Not to mention, his penchant for jumping into the fray and refusing to back down had earned him an inside look at Pip's life. He had learned more about Pip in one afternoon with the guys than he imagined he would pull from Pip in a month. It turned out Pip hadn't been one hundred percent honest. While he was a caretaker slash companion, it was his mom he sat with each day. Savage didn't blame Pip for not admitting to being tied to this much money. Savage understood what it was like to only be wanted for who he was and what he could give.

Pip hadn't been home yet when Savage had turned up earlier than expected. The behemoths who met him at the door were all Pip's family in some fashion or another. They were all also mountain-sized and protective as hell. They had immediately started pushing Savage's buttons and testing his mettle. Savage lowkey loved that Pip had this huge and overbearing family keeping an eye on him. Pip obviously needed people protecting him. That knowledge was abundantly apparent as Savage stepped from the shower and into Pip's bedroom. Pip looked innocent as hell while sitting on the bed, waiting for Savage. His gaze turned Savage's way as Savage came through the door wearing nothing more than a towel. Pip's gorgeous, almost yellow eyes followed Savage's every move. He looked guileless as hell. Savage wanted to ruin him for all others. He couldn't explain his feelings. Savage had never experienced even the smallest desire to settle down, and he had just met this guy. There were a lot of weird things about this entire situation. Savage felt how he felt, and he wasn't one to deny himself anything.

As Savage crossed the room, a flush rose on Pip's cheeks. Savage had been to the top of his profession, gaining the highest accolades and achieving dreams beyond even his imagination. Yet, somehow, he felt even more powerful in that moment than he did when he won his matches. Pip was a prize that Savage had a feeling no one had ever won.

Savage stood over Pip. Pip's gaze lifted but didn't quite meet Savage's eyes. "You're sitting on my clothes."

Pip blushed. "Oh." He tried moving.

Savage set his hands on Pip's shoulders, stopping him. "I have a question."

"Okay." Pip finally met his stare.

A drop of water fell from Savage's hair. Pip's gaze shifted that way. The water hit Savage's shoulder and rolled down his torso. Pip's gaze followed the droplet. Before Savage could find a way to pose his question correctly, Pip shot forward and caught the bead of water on his tongue. He didn't stop there. He lapped at Savage's skin at the edge of his towel. Pip's tongue felt amazing. A pant escaped Savage. He went hard. Savage never would have dreamed that such a strange move could make him so fucking hot. He buried his fingers in Pip's hair and held on. Pip's hair was so soft, Savage had the sudden urge to pet him. Savage shifted positions, hoping to urge Pip closer to where he wanted that mouth to go. The bedroom door flew open so hard, it bounced against the wall.

Savage jumped away without thought. His heart tried leaping from his chest. Even though he had no reason to feel guilty, he did.

A guy Savage hadn't met stood in the open bedroom doorway. He was young and blue-eyed. A bright smile stretched his lips. "Get dressed. We're having a bonfire party."

As quickly as the guy arrived, he disappeared.

Savage's gaze moved Pip's way. "Who the fuck was that?"

Pip looked dazed and turned on. Savage wanted to tackle him to the bed. Pip stared at Savage's body like he wanted to get taken down. "Um." Pip licked his lips. "Evan."

"I thought Evan was the wolf."

Pip blinked. He didn't answer right away. Savage fought a smirk. He was the one who had scattered Pip's thoughts. Pip was his. "Baptiste named the wolf Evan after the Evan you just met because they're so much alike," Pip finally said, sounding like his mind was still only half on the conversation.

Savage latched on to the subject, hoping to cool his lust. "Who is Baptiste?"

"Evan's... boss."

Savage nodded. He didn't care about Baptiste or his connection to Evan—the man or wolf. He simply needed to lose the hard-on.

Pip stood and moved to the open doorway. "I guess I should head out back with everyone else and let you dress."

Savage dropped his towel.

Pip closed the door.

They stared at each other in silence. Savage decided to be the one to break it. "Are you a virgin?" He had to know. Pip did way too much blushing for someone with much experience. Not to mention, he had behemoth brothers standing between Pip and anyone wanting in Pip's pants, namely Savage.

For once, Pip didn't blush. "Yes."

Shit. Savage couldn't fuck a virgin in the five minutes they had to get outside with Pip's family.

He moved to the bed and started dressing.

"Did I turn you off that quickly?"

Savage had his underwear half up his thighs when Pip's hurt-sounding question felt like it punched him in the face. In an instant, he was across the room, pinning Pip against the closed door. With his tongue in Pip's mouth, he led Pip's hand to his erection, leaving Pip no room to doubt his desire.

He pulled away enough to press his forehead against Pip's. "I've never wanted anyone this much in my life. But when I take you, it won't be some quick fuck against the wall while your family waits outside. It'll be torturously slow. You'll beg for release. When I'm done, you'll never want anyone else."

Pip drew a ragged-sounding breath. "I already don't want anyone else."

Something tugged inside Savage's chest. He felt closer to Pip than any other soul on the planet. It didn't make sense, but Savage felt something for Pip. He needed to be the only man for Pip. Savage whisked his lips across Pip's, craving the sweetness of Pip's attention. "You're not allowed to date anyone else. You're with me now."

An adorable smile snapped to Pip's lips. "Okay. Ditto."

Never. Not one time in his life had Savage let a person tie him down. He had been waiting for Pip. "Deal." He sealed the promise with a kiss. Savage pulled away before things got too heated. "Go be with your family before I change my mind about that slow lovemaking. I'll get dressed and meet you outside."

With a nod, Pip slipped from the room, leaving

Savage with a swamp of pre-cum in his underwear and an entire night of no alone time ahead of him. A smile that felt wicked pulled at his lips. He only had to make it a few more hours and then he would coax Pip into his bed. Goddamn. Savage was scared as hell. Pip really might be the one.

WOLVES, A TIGER, A DRUID, VAMPIRES, at least two gods, and a Nephilim all wearing human skin milled around the fire. Tam and Evan had dragged out their cauldron too. They promised it was only hunch punch inside, but still. Pip had no idea how he would keep Savage from learning the truth before Pip figured out how to tell him about the supernatural world living in the shadows of his human existence.

Jonathan moved to stand beside Pip. He rubbed Pip's back. "It's okay, sweetie. Everyone knows how important it is to meet your mate. We won't mess this up. See how good I'm being? I even forced my wings away tonight. My back itches like crazy and I probably won't be able to stay long tonight, but no one wants to ruin this for you."

Pip felt terrible. This was Jonathan's home. He shouldn't have to hide. Pip knew how hard appearing human was for Jonathan, but Pip hadn't decided how to handle things yet. Then Savage appeared with a drink in each hand. He held a cup out to Pip and Pip forgot why he cared about anything other than the man hovering over him.

Savage's gaze moved Jonathan's way.

Jonathan stopped rubbing Pip's back and held his hands up for Savage to see. "Don't get jealous. I'm Pip's nephew."

A line appeared between Savage's eyebrows. "You have my attention."

Pip nearly groaned. All this storytelling would eventually catch up to him.

Jonathan had no trouble jumping right in. "Celeste is my grandmother. When she adopted Pip, he became my uncle."

Pip supposed that was true.

Savage nodded. "I'll admit I'm having a hard time figuring out everyone's connection to Pip."

Jonathan made a show of looking at everyone there. He was quite the actor. "I started to say that everyone here is related to Pip in some way, but then thought better of it. Now that I'm looking around, though, it's true. Everyone here is family in some way or another. Be it by marriage or whatnot." He met Savage's gaze again. "I hope you're not easily offended or judgmental. This is a rough bunch and I'm not the only one here who has two husbands."

Savage's eyebrows rose. A surprised-sounding laugh burst from him. "Hey, whatever. You gotta live your life."

Pip bit the inside of his cheek. Savage was trying so hard to take things in stride. Pip was proud to be with him.

Jonathan's gaze slid past Savage and locked on to his husbands by the fire. His expression changed, turning almost hungry. "Speaking of which, I should get back to them." Without a word, Jonathan walked away and joined Cin and Niall. The pair immediately squished Jonathan between them in a heated exchange Pip had to look away from.

Pip cleared his throat. "Sorry about my family."

Savage laughed. The sound caused chill bumps to skirt across Pip's skin. "Don't apologize. I think they're amazing. You got really lucky, getting adopted into this family. They're a little weird, but in a good way—like Robinson family strange."

Pip stared at Savage, unsure of how to react. "I don't know who that is."

Savage's smile grew. "It's a Disney movie. You know, *Meet the Robinsons*. It's got the T-Rex that's like, 'I've got a big head and little arms.' You've really never seen that movie?"

Pip couldn't explain why he couldn't stop smiling. Savage had acted out the T-Rex's movie quote, drawing his arms in and making them look short.

Pip genuinely enjoyed Savage's company. "I haven't seen it. Maybe we can watch it together sometime."

The affront in Savage's expression melted away. "I'd like that."

Pip sipped the drink Savage handed him. He curled his nose as liquor hit his tongue.

A sexy chuckle rumbled from Savage. "That bad, huh?"

"I'm not a drinker," Pip confessed around the burn.

Savage's mouth lifted in one corner, making him look like a naughty kid. "I'll trade you for my water if I can stay the night."

"You got water and I got this. No fair." Pip switched cups with him and gratefully washed the taste of liquor from his tongue while Savage tried the punch.

"Holy shit. That's awful. Give me back the water." They both laughed while trading cups again. Savage's eyes shone bright with good humor. "Would you like to get out of here? I'd planned to take you on a proper date tonight, but we can do whatever you'd like."

"I'm actually pretty hungry," Pip admitted. "It looks like the guys just plan to drink tonight. I'm pretty boring. I'd rather eat."

Savage's stomach growled. He laughed as he pressed his hand to his stomach. "I'm starving. Name the place."

"I'm a huge fan of Truman's shrimp, but it's only a to-go place."

Savage's eyes flashed with wicked intent. "That's perfect. We can take it back to my place."

Pip took Savage's cup and set it on the ground alongside his. He knew they would get magicked away later. "Let's go."

"Do you need to tell anyone you're going?"

Pip shook his head. "Nope. We just have to be quick, so we don't get guilted into staying."

Savage looked around. Pip felt Savage's mischievousness build a half second before he found himself over Savage's shoulder. A laugh stuck in Pip's throat as Savage made a run for it. At the passenger side of Savage's truck, he barely slowed before tossing Pip inside. Savage looked his way with laughter in his eyes as he climbed behind the wheel. "Damn, darling. You're light as a feather. I definitely need to get you something to eat."

Pip snapped his seatbelt in place. "I'm yours to do with as you please."

Savage's smile slipped away. Heat flashed in his eyes. "Yeah. You are."

Pip felt that promise all the way to his soul. He couldn't wait for more.

Chapter Three

Pip was an unstoppable force of endless energy. He made Savage feel younger than he had in years. A few years back, Savage had built a training center in his home for doing workouts outside of his training with Ace. It was the only way to stop people from posting photos of his workouts online. Plus, no one else seemed to have the exact thing he wanted to get the most from his time spent training. Part of his home gym was a climbing zone with trampoline floors. That way, he could fall with little to no risk of injury.

While touring the house, Pip had taken one look at the training center and lost his mind. While Savage had always seen the space in his house as a place to work, Pip had turned it into a fun zone. He had dragged Savage into the room, bouncing and flipping. Savage had witnessed Pip's perfect balance in the parking lot of the arena. This was different. Pip was like a kid. He made Savage feel like one too.

Happiness flashed in Pip's eyes. "Why do you ever leave your house? This place is great."

"If I never left my house, I wouldn't have met you." Savage crowded Pip's space. They were both sweaty from playing. That didn't stop Savage from wrapping his arms around Pip's waist.

"That's true, I guess."

Savage kissed the shell of Pip's ear because he couldn't stop himself. There was something about Pip. He made Savage want to touch him. Be with him. "I honestly can't recall the last time I just enjoyed the day the way I have today. Thank you for that."

Pip looked up at him with puppy dog eyes. "You should enjoy yourself more often. You have a gorgeous smile."

"You're gorgeous."

Pip blushed.

Savage's heart couldn't take it. "What's with all the blushing every time I compliment you? You act like no one has ever told you how sexy you are, and I can't believe that. I swear you damn near broke my concentration last night just by sitting ringside. Do you know how embarrassing it would have been if I had lost the fight because I couldn't stop staring at you?"

Pip's face got redder by the second. "Stop. Not everyone is like you. Some of us are just normal people who never get praised."

Savage's smile slipped away. He understood loneliness. That was what he saw in Pip's eyes. "There's nothing normal about you. I think you're extraordinary."

"You're tired."

Savage was taken aback by the sudden change in topic. "Between your family challenging my manliness and this, yeah, a bit. I'm not too tired for you, though."

Pip's gaze moved over Savage's face, as if searching for something only he could see. He shook his head. "No. You're soul weary."

Savage's lips parted in surprise. He didn't know what to say. No one had ever seen him so well. Pip was amazingly intuitive. "I suppose I am."

Pip looked adorably shy for a minute, sending Savage's curiosity through the roof. "Maybe you could hold me for a while, and you'd feel better."

There was no way Savage could turn down that adorable offer. "How do you feel about taking a shower with me and then me holding you all night?"

The bashful expressions were killing Savage. "Okay."

It took every ounce of Savage's willpower not to scoop Pip from the floor and run for the bathroom. Instead, he took Pip's hand and headed toward his bedroom. Savage measured his pace, hoping not to seem as desperate as he felt.

"You have such a gorgeous house," Pip said as they passed through the bedroom and into the en suite. Savage had bought the house based on the bathroom alone. One side of the room was a wet room. It was glass enclosed with shower heads and jets and a free-standing tub inside. The space was perfect for whatever purpose he chose. Tonight, this spot was where he planned to seduce Pip.

Savage dropped Pip's hand and moved the shower's computer panel to set his heat, steam, and pressure settings. He turned and found Pip naked and waiting. Pip didn't look the least bit embarrassed of his nudity. It was like he was in his natural state. Thank god, because Pip should never cover his body again. He was delicious. Pip's entire body was firm and sleek. Savage's lust doubled.

While holding Pip's stare, Savage peeled his shirt up and over his head. He tossed it aside before going to work on his pants. Pip never looked away. Savage finished stripping, letting Pip see his arousal. As Savage looked on, Pip went hard. Savage lost his breath. Pip made him feel powerful and sexy. Savage opened the glass door and stepped inside. He held the door open, enticing Pip to join him. Despite Pip's usual blushing, he didn't hesitate to cross the room and step inside the shower with Savage.

The wall inside the wet room was one huge window, giving him a view of the pool. There was no chance of being seen by anyone. His yard was surrounded by a thick line of trees and then followed by fencing before backing onto protected land. He could do whatever he wanted with no chance of being seen. Still, the spot gave the illusion of being watched.

Pip moved to the window and looked out. The lights inside and surrounding the pool made the blue glimmering spot look gorgeous in the dark. "I love this."

Savage closed the distance between them and drew Pip back against his chest. He was tired of waiting. His hand slid south until he reached Pip's cock. He stroked. The sexiest ragged breath he had ever heard escaped Pip. Pip's head fell forward, leaving his nape exposed for Savage's teeth. Savage scraped his teeth across the newly exposed skin. Pip flattened his palms against the glass.

"Damn." The word slipped from Savage without thought. It was pulled from his chest by pure lust. He had never had anyone surrender to him the way Pip did. Pip made Savage want to show him a night in which he would never recover. He wanted Pip to keep crawling back and begging for more. Savage had a darker side that needed to be fed. Pip checked every goddamn box.

"Don't move." Savage could hear the way his

voice had deepened. It was too late to go back now. He went to work, pleasuring Pip. He tugged and stroked. "If your hands leave that window, I'll stop."

Pip didn't make a single sound. He stayed perfectly still—like prey hiding from its hunter.

Savage rolled his hips, letting Pip feel his erection between their bodies. "I'm going to fuck you, Pip. But not yet." An evil-sounding chuckle fell from Savage's lips. His dark side was on display now. "First, I want you to paint this window with your cum. Then, when you're trying to catch your breath, that's when you're mine."

"I'm always yours."

Savage sucked in a breath. He felt Pip's claim in his heart. This wasn't bullshit talk in the heat of the moment. Pip would ride with him through any-thing. "Fuck yeah." He pulled Pip's hair and dragged his head back. "You are." He claimed Pip's mouth, biting at his lips and sucking his tongue. Savage treated Pip's dick like he would his own, go-ing for maximum pleasure. He swore he could feel the tension rising in Pip. Savage wanted him to be as relaxed as possible. He wanted to zap the energy from Pip's body so he would take whatever Savage gave him. Savage wasn't a gentle lover. He could pet Pip and spoil him. Savage couldn't fuck him gently, though. He wasn't built like that.

Pip moaned against Savage's lips.

Savage pumped faster.

Still, Pip obeyed Savage's command to keep his palms flattened against the window. He whim-pered around Savage's tongue. Something dark and possessive grew in Savage's chest. It got bigger every second he spent with Pip. Savage had always been a loner. He had found the one he wanted to sit with him. This was his man. Savage would kill for him.

Pip cried out. He shook in Savage's arms. Savage kissed him sweetly, silently vowing to keep him safe. He would be Pip's protector, shielding his innocent nature from the harsh world, but he would still fuck him like he hated him.

"Stay," Savage demanded against Pip's lips. As much as it killed him, he pulled away and left Pip behind. He moved to the tub and turned on the water. As the tub filled, Savage dropped in a few bath bombs. Whoever had staged the house had put a few rubber ducks on the top cutout space meant for towels and washcloths. He had left them there, and his cleaning crew kept everything fresh. Savage knew now why he hadn't gotten rid of them. He grabbed one along with a couple of washcloths. Savage draped the washcloths over the edge of the tub and tossed the rubber duck in before returning to Pip's side. He hadn't moved.

"Good boy."

Savage wanted to praise Pip and baby him. Pip deserved all the pampering for the fucking he would soon receive. Savage swept Pip into his arms and carried him to the tub. He lowered Pip until he was a few inches away from the water.

"Feel of the water, angel."

Pip dragged his fingers across the bubbly multi-colored pool that waited for him.

"Is it too hot?"

Pip shook his head. "It's perfect."

74

"Good." Damn. Savage couldn't believe how deep his voice sounded in his possessive hunger. He lowered Pip into the water. "Enjoy. Get clean. I'm about to make you really fucking dirty."

Pip looked up at him with such hope in his eyes that Savage's knees nearly buckled. Savage had never encountered anyone so naively seductive. Savage grabbed the shampoo and scrubbed his own hair before passing the bottle to Pip. His gaze stayed locked on Pip while Savage showered. Savage scrubbed every inch, giving Pip a show. After getting clean, Pip sat in the bathtub, squeezing the rubber duck and staring at Savage like Savage was the best part of a movie. As much as Savage wanted to blow for Pip, he didn't want it to be like this. He had to get Pip in bed.

"Are you clean?"

Pip nodded.

An unnatural-sounding growl rumbled in Savage's throat. "Then let the water out of the tub, baby boy."

Pip nodded and did as told while Savage shut down the steam and shower. He grabbed a towel and headed Pip's way.

"Stand up."

Pip stood. He still held the rubber duck.

Savage let him keep it. He wrapped the towel around Pip and lifted him from the tub.

"I keep this place cold, so it might be a little chilly on the way to the bed. Don't worry. You won't notice for long."

"You'll keep me warm."

The trust Pip showed in him fed Savage's darkness. His greed grew. "Exactly." Savage's long stride ate up the floor between the bathroom and his bed. At the edge of the mattress, he shifted Pip's weight to one arm and pulled down the covers. Pip held his stare as Savage lowered him onto the bed. Savage grabbed the lube and some condoms before climbing in and straddling Pip's body. He kept his weight balanced on his knees so he wouldn't flatten Pip. Pip was still hard. Savage stroked him in be-tween putting on a condom and lubing the outside.

He shifted positions, widening Pip's thighs and settling down in between them. Savage lubed Pip's asshole, stretching him. "Do you plan to keep that rubber duck?"

Pip nodded. "I like it." He put in his mouth and bit.

A chuckle that sounded evil even to Savage fell from Savage's lips. "Good idea." He impaled Pip with his cock.

Pip's fingers dug into Savage's arms. He whimpered.

Savage held still inside Pip while massaging Pip's erection. He felt Pip's muscles slowly relax. His breathing slowed as his body accepted Savage's intrusion. Savage rocked a little, testing the waters. Pip turned his head, spit out the rubber duck, and panted. Savage thrust a little harder. A soft moan vibrated from Pip. Savage lost his shit. His thin veneer of civility fell away. Savage scooped Pip from the mattress so he could hold him at the perfect angle, and then he fucked him. The humanity seeped away. Savage bit and licked while pounding inside Pip. Pip didn't try to get away or protest. He moaned and gasped while Savage treated him like a toy. He used Pip's body, taking his pleasure. There was no thought to comfort. He wanted the hot hole that sucked at his dick. Savage craved the blinding ecstasy. He needed the release. Pip cried Savage's name and tore at his skin. Cum streaked across Savage's abs, turning him even more crazed. The pressure climbing his shaft couldn't be held at bay as Pip's orgasm seemed to feed his. He swore he physically felt Pip's release. A roar ripped from Savage's throat as his body exploded into waves of soul-rocking pleasure. He held Pip in a bruising embrace while he ate at Pip's mouth, needing to taste Pip's tongue while he enjoyed his ass.

The darkness bled from Savage. He gently lowered Pip to the mattress and sank into him. While Savage was careful not to crush Pip, he also didn't give him any space. Their kiss turned loving. Their palms flattened against each other's before their fingers linked. Savage held on while his heart tried climbing from his chest and into Pip's. He felt closer to Pip than he ever had with anyone. It wasn't the sex talking. He had lived long and hard enough to spot the moments that would change him. Pip was meant to be an important chapter of his life. He didn't know why Pip had been sent into his life, but Savage would cherish him and protect him. This one was his. Savage would keep him safe.

Chapter Four

THE CHILLY AIR SMELLED UNFAMILIAR until Pip caught Savage's scent. Beneath the mound of covers, Pip rooted around, searching for the owner of such a delicious smell. He found Savage's side of the bed empty. Pip poked his nose out and sniffed. The air smelled clean, but that was it. He uncovered his head and listened. Nothing. His clothes were still in the bathroom. Pip didn't want to put them on. He wasn't a huge fan of wearing clothes. One of Savage's t-shirts was on the floor. Pip grabbed it and tossed it on before going in search of Savage. The t-shirt fell to Pip's knees. It was comfortable as far as clothes went and smelled like Savage. Pip kind of wanted to keep it. He caught Savage's scent and followed. Pip spotted Savage in a large room that looked like an office. He was on the phone. Savage looked up and focused on Pip lingering in the hall. He motioned for Pip to come inside before patting his knee. Pip scrambled inside and onto Savage's lap. Savage kissed Pip's forehead while listening to the voice on the other end. Pip felt like his soul settled into its happy place as he settled into Savage's arms.

"I don't know what to tell you, Ace. Before my last fight, I told you it would be the last for a while. Maybe forever. I haven't decided yet."

Pip tilted his chin up and stared at Savage's face while Savage spoke. It wasn't that he tried to eavesdrop, but he was right there.

Savage let out an annoyed-sounding sigh. "Yeah. That's fine. Just leave me registered. You know I don't care if the USADA shows up to test me. I've got nothing to hide."

Pip shifted higher and licked Savage's neck. He couldn't stop himself. His mate's scent called to him.

A soft pant escaped Savage.

Pip smiled against Savage's throat.

"Okay. I'll drop by later. We'll talk then."

Savage tossed the phone aside and held Pip tighter, squeezing him. "Good morning, sexy. Did I wake you up when I left?"

Pip shook his head while inhaling Savage's scent. "I woke up on my own and missed you." Pip didn't know how to be normal or what human couples did. It was possible he was too clingy, and people didn't usually crawl all over other people. Pip couldn't help it. Savage was his person. Pip wanted cuddles.

Savage's hand found its way beneath the t-shirt. He squeezed Pip's bare ass. "Damn. You're such a temptation. I wish I didn't have anything to do today other than to take you back to bed. Unfortunately, I have to swing by the gym and iron some things out with Ace. Since you don't have any clothes here, we'll have to swing by your place first. That cuts down on our time."

Pip fought the urge to pout. Savage had a life outside of him. Thankfully, Savage wasn't talking about dumping him on Jonathan's doorstep and never looking back. Pip would take what he could get. "Sounds good."

Savage kept stroking him—like he was in no hurry to go anywhere. "Do you have to work today? It didn't even occur to me that you might have something else going on. I'm just keeping you like

I have the right."

He did have the right. "Celeste will call me if she needs me."

Savage didn't respond right away. He sat in silence while rubbing Pip's back, as if lost in thought. Pip could feel the questions rising inside Savage. Finally, he broke. "Why do you call your mom by her name?"

Pip rearranged himself in Savage's lap so he could meet Savage's gaze as he spoke. "If you knew her, you would not be asking that question," Pip answered with a laugh. "Celeste is very powerful." Pip realized what he said and tried backpedaling. "I mean personality-wise. I love her. She is always Mom in my heart, and sometimes I call her Mom at home, but I assure you she would tell me if I should call her Mom all the time." By the time Pip finished his speech, Savage wore a gorgeous smile.

"I can hear how much you love her."

Pip had to change the subject. No good could come of him talking about his life. "What about your mom? What's she like?"

Savage's smile faltered. "She died a long time ago."

Pip's heart squeezed. He could feel Savage's pain. "And your dad?"

Bitterness etched Savage's features. "He disappeared an even longer time ago."

Pip understood. He had been created by a goddess that had then abandoned him. There had been many years Pip had spent alone. An unfortunate number of gods and goddesses created life for the sake of creation. They didn't foster that life and watch it flourish. It was about having pretty things.

They didn't love the life they created. Celeste did. Still, those years without love or meaning haunted Pip, making him needy and bitter. The anger in his chest caught and held Pip's attention. His gaze met Savage's. Pip realized it was Savage's emotions he felt. There was darkness inside Savage. Pip kind of wanted to touch it. Savage was his mate. He knew he needed to claim him or the desperation between them would become unbearable. It was odd how much Pip enjoyed the anticipation. He half expected Savage to hurt him... in a good way. Savage's eyebrow rose. Just the one. Pip knew—whether Savage realized it or not—he had heard Pip's thoughts. Savage smirked. He had Pip's number.

"Oh, baby. I need to take you to pack your bags before you get me in trouble."

Pip played innocent. "Why am I packing a

bag?"

Savage stood and tossed Pip over his shoulder. "I've decided to keep you."

Pip hid his face against Savage's back. "Okay."

A delicious growl vibrated from Savage. "Why do you feel like you're blushing? I'm pretty sure you were five seconds away from begging me to choke you while I fuck you. Now I can feel your hot face against my back over me saying I want you to stay with me for a while. You are a conundrum."

An unsteady breath stuttered from Pip's lungs at the thought of Savage choking him. He didn't think Savage would hurt him for real, but he swore he could already feel Savage's fingers holding him in place by his neck.

Savage stopped. The air seemed to thicken. He shifted Pip into his arms and slowly lowered him until Pip sat on the edge of the bed. Savage's expression matched his name. Pip wasn't the least bit afraid. He wanted whatever came next.

"I'm not one you should toy with, baby boy. I'll put you in a collar."

As a wild animal, that should have been the most terrifying statement anyone had ever said to him. Instead, a pant escaped Pip.

In a flash, Pip found himself on his back with Savage's huge body pinning him to the bed. His fingers encircled Pip's throat, but he didn't squeeze. "You should run."

"Make me." Goddess help him. The taunt fell from Pip's lips without any thought to how deep he kept sinking.

An evil-sounding chuckle fell from Savage's

lips and seemed to reverberate from the walls. Savage sat back on his heels and stared down at Pip. "Ace can wait."

At the threat in Savage's tone, Pip realized he might have gone too far. Chills ran down his spine. He tried scrambling away. Savage snagged Pip around the waist before he could escape. With a flip, Pip found himself facedown. Before he could regain any traction, wet fingers probed his asshole. Pip fell still and moaned. A solid slap landed across his ass cheek.

Savage squeezed. "I see you're in the mood to tease." Savage smacked Pip's ass again.

It didn't hurt. It felt kind of good. Pip pretended to try to get away again, testing a theory. Savage swatted his ass again. Another moan rose in his throat. He hadn't imagined things. It felt good.

"I thought to give you time to recover." Savage toyed with Pip's asshole, making him feel even better. "But I see now that you can't wait for more attention." An even bigger intrusion stretched Pip's hole. Savage's voice turned guttural as he pressed deeper inside Pip. "If you need to get fucked again, I'm here for it. I'll always have what you need, baby boy." Savage's fingers encircled Pip's throat. He dragged Pip up and back against his chest.

Something expanded inside Pip's chest. He felt his ownership passing to Savage. Savage didn't hurt him. He controlled him. It was empowering and freeing. Pip had new boundaries, but he knew Savage would keep him safe as he allowed Pip to have everything. Pip had always been spoiled. He had always been a pet. This was different. He could feel the darkness in Savage churning alongside his need to own and protect Pip. Pip felt even more special than he thought he would with a mate. He instinctively knew their relationship wouldn't be a normal one. Savage needed something a little more. He needed someone to make him feel special—like he owned a slice of heaven. Pip was a godling. He was a small piece of the heavens. Pip was the only one who could give Savage what he needed to thrive. It was the most powerful feeling in the world. He was more than paired with Savage as a mate. They made each other more.

Savage shifted positions and hit at the perfect angle. A moan tore from Pip's throat.

Savage's hold tightened on Pip's neck, keeping him in place. "That's it. I have everything you need. Stay focused on me. Don't feel anything but my dick. You have no idea how much pleasure I could give you. I don't want to break you. I want you willing to crawl to me when you need what only I can give you."

Pip kept his eyes closed and concentrated solely on Savage. He felt every place they touched inside and out. The urge to bite and claim Savage forever was powerful. His teeth itched. Pip didn't get a chance to bite. Savage shoved him forward, pressing Pip's face into the mattress before pounding inside Pip. Every ounce of his attention locked on the ecstasy. He scratched at the covers as Savage stole an orgasm from Pip. There was no slow build. One second, he had been considering claiming his mate. The next, he was ass up and screaming Savage's name. Savage took no mercy. He dragged every twitch of pleasure from Pip, addicting Pip to his touch. Pip hadn't known. He had spent too much time in the heavens, where emotions and sensations were muted. Pip couldn't have understood what he missed. Savage would show him. He would make Pip understand. In return, Pip would soften Savage's life. He would bring Savage peace. As soon as Savage got past Pip being a fox part of the time, that was. That could be a problem.

SAVAGE WAS LOWKEY CONVINCED Pip had been sent by the devil to test him. Everything about the guy was perfection. Savage was a jealous, possessive bastard. Someone perfect like Pip got noticed a lot. At the gym, Savage had left Pip alone for literally five minutes with a candy bar to occupy him, because—for fuck's sake—for someone as tiny as Pip, he ate a lot. He wanted a meal and Savage needed to get some shit worked out with Ace. Somehow, in the five minutes Savage had been missing, this asshole gym rat, Steve, had Pip cornered. Savage could hear him harassing Pip from across the room.

"Come on, man. You have to work off that candy."

Pip looked nervous. "No, thank you."

Savage was fucking furious. He had no idea how Steve suggested Pip work off the calories of his candy bar. It didn't matter. No one made Pip uncomfortable.

Steve wasn't done. "I'll take it easy on you the first time."

Savage growled. His long stride ate up the floor until he stood half an inch away from chest bumping the dude's back until he hit the ground.

"Who in the fuck do you think you're talking to?"

The guy scrambled away a few feet as he turned to find Savage hovering over him. No doubt Savage looked every bit as ready to tear off Steve's head as he felt. "Hey, Savage. I was trying to talk this guy into signing up to train here."

Savage felt his features harden. He imagined he looked as deadly as he felt. No one bruised his baby's skin. "That's my baby boy. He doesn't fight. He looks pretty and gets pet. But if you feel the need to get your neck snapped in the ring, I'll be glad to do it." By the time Savage finished his threat, his nostrils flared, and he spoke through clenched teeth.

Pip flashed him a sweet smile.

Steve held up his hands in surrender. "I wasn't trying to start a fight."

Savage's temper didn't cool. "You still found one."

"I'm hungry."

The sweet reminder zapped the fury from Savage. His gaze swung Pip's way.

Pip gave him puppy dog eyes. "Can we get shrimp?"

Savage swept Steve out of the way. "We had shrimp last night, baby."

Pip nodded. "Oh. Okay."

"If you want shrimp, I'll get you shrimp."

A smile exploded across Pip's face. "Yay. Can we go now or are you fighting?"

Steve scrambled away.

"We can go now."

Pip practically skipped out the door, obviously happy to finally be getting fed. As he climbed in the truck, a look of confusion touched his features. "That was weird. I've never had anyone insinuate that I'm fat before. Maybe I should skip lunch."

Savage stood in the open doorway, waiting for Pip to put on his seatbelt. He fought an inner battle. On one hand, he couldn't believe Pip didn't realize Steve had been flirting with him and Savage didn't know if he wanted Pip to figure it out. On the other, he couldn't have Pip skipping meals. In the end, he had to be honest.

"That guy was trying to get you in the ring so he could touch you. It had nothing to do with your weight. You're perfect. He's just the kind of guy who is too chickenshit to say he wants a man, so he gets his rocks off by putting the men he wants in uncomfortable positions under the guise of training them."

Pip slowly nodded. "Oh. Okay. You were right to be mad. He's not a good person."

Savage fought the urge to run his tongue over his teeth. He still wanted to feel Steve's bones crush beneath his hands. "No. He's not." Savage's gaze slid back toward the building. Maybe he still had time...

Pip leaned out and kissed Savage's ear. "We don't have to get shrimp if you don't want. I'm bad about eating the same things all the time until I'm sick of it, and then I never want to eat it again."

The darkness bled from Savage. His gaze slid back Pip's way. "No. I can order myself something different. You're getting shrimp." He checked Pip's seat belt. Even Savage didn't know why he couldn't stop being overprotective for five seconds. All he knew was that he had found the one for him. Now

Savage had to protect Pip from the ugly side of the world. That meant Steve had to go.

Chapter Five

THEY WERE HAVING SALMON FOR the third time this week. Savage had no complaints. After four months of dating and spending every second together, Savage was accustomed to Pip's oddities. In fact, he found a lot of comfort in Pip's consistency. Pip ate, played, cuddled, and submitted. He was everything Savage needed to survive. Savage didn't understand why he wanted Pip more and more every day like he had never had him. While Savage understood the unnatural, it seemed some desperation for Pip should have passed by now. Instead, it grew stronger every day.

Pip squirmed in his seat.

Savage bit back a smile. Pip was always too restless to sit at the kitchen table for too long. "Take off your shirt."

A grateful smile touched Pip's lips. He took off his shirt. Savage didn't understand Pip's aversion to clothes, but he wouldn't force Pip to be uncomfortable. Since Pip had food, which always made him happy, Savage knew Pip had something else bothering him. He started with the basics.

"Feel free to take off your pants too, if your clothes are bothering you."

A knowing smile touched Pip's lips. He took a sip of his water before standing. Savage leaned back in his chair and watched as Pip's hands went to the button on his jeans. Pip moved slowly, leaving no room for doubt this was a show. He slid down his zipper. Savage's hunger stirred. This was life with Pip. Everything was in excess. He always felt starved. One hip bared and then the other. Savage's phone rang. Normally, he wouldn't ignore Pip for anyone. It was Ace, and Ace only called without texting first if there was an emergency.

Savage pushed his plate aside and answered his call on speaker. He needed his hands. "Hello?"

"Hey, Savage. Have you seen the news?"

Savage motioned for Pip to take off his pants. Then he tapped the spot on the table where he expected Pip to sit. "There's nothing happening in the world I care to hear about."

"In this case, it pertains to you. The training center burned down last night. One of the guys got trapped inside. It might be some time before I get another place set up for us to train."

Savage fought to keep the satisfaction from his expression. "That's fine."

Pip looked unsure since Ace sounded dis-
traught.

Savage tapped the spot on the table again.
"Who was trapped inside?" Savage already knew,
but whatever. He had to sound like he cared, but he
didn't intend to see Ace again. It had come that time
again in his long existence. He needed to disappear.
Savage just hadn't quite decided what to do with Pip
yet. Obviously, Pip had to come too, but that was a
conversation he hadn't decided how to start.

Pip sat.

"It was that Steve guy. The one who was a little
handsy."

Well, Savage had to let some time pass. Otherwise, people would have gotten suspicious if he
snapped Steve's neck after publicly arguing with

him. "I don't know how to respond to this one without sounding like a terrible person, so I'm sorry about your training center. Will insurance cover everything?"

"Yeah. I'll be fine. I just wanted to touch base with you. The last thing I want is to lose you to another trainer."

Savage snagged Pip's hips and hauled him to the edge of the table. He licked Pip's cock before responding. "That won't happen." It really wouldn't. Savage would have to hide for a while so people forgot him. He tongued Pip's dick, getting him hard.

"That's good to hear. I'll keep you posted."

"Sounds good. Have a great night." Savage sucked Pip's crown.

"You too, Savage. See you soon."

Savage tapped the face of his phone, disconnecting the call. He smiled when Pip immediately moaned like he had been holding it in.

Pip still tried to hold a conversation while Savage enjoyed his meal. "Are you okay? I know that place was important to you."

"It's just a building and I'm done boxing. It's our time now." He swore he could feel Pip bubbling with more questions. Savage swallowed Pip's cock, ensuring he forgot each and every one. To his surprise and delight, Pip didn't submit. He pushed Savage away and picked up a crystal bottle of oil from the center of the table.

"Is this safe to use?"

Savage didn't play dumb. Savage knew what Pip wanted to do with that oil. He liked it when Pip didn't turn shy. "Yes."

Pip poured a few drops on his fingers and taunted Savage with the vision of him toying with his own asshole. Savage's gaze moved to the hundred-thousand-dollar collar he had snapped around Pip's neck nearly three months ago. He never got tired of showing off his property. Savage hooked his finger through the ring of diamonds on Pip's collar. He tugged, pulling Pip closer. The darkness churned inside him, wanting to be fed. "You're teasing the wrong one, baby boy. Come fuck me, if you want me." He released Pip and leaned back in his chair. Savage watched as Pip slipped from the table and went to work on Savage's jeans. Savage didn't help. If Pip wanted sex over a blow job, he could take it. Triumph lit Pip's eyes as he set Savage's dick free. Savage loved watching Pip blossom. Pip looked a little less sure of himself as he tried straddling Savage's lap at the right angle to get what he wanted. He had an adorable line between his eyebrows.

"Pip."

Pip's expression cleared as he met Savage's stare. "What?"

"Ask me for what you want."

"Will you make love to me, please?"

It was such a sweet-sounding request that Savage exploded from his seat. In a flash, he had Pip back on the table and was buried inside him. He thrust while kissing and biting every place he could reach. Savage sucked, bringing the blood to the surface of Pip's skin, leaving hickeys behind. Pip scratched at Savage's skin, crying out for more. Savage pulled Pip into his arms and straightened. Pip was so light; Savage had no trouble using Pip's body like a toy. He rolled his hips while lifting and lowering Pip's body, taking his pleasure. With his head thrown back, Pip moaned and cried, begging for more. Cum coated the space between their bodies, as proof of how quickly he could make Pip come. It wasn't enough. Savage wanted to crawl up inside Pip's ass and stay there all night. He headed for the bedroom and climbed into bed. With Pip sitting on his hips, Savage thrust upward while pulling Pip down. He was insane with need. He felt Pip's second orgasm. Cum hit his bottom lip. Savage licked it away as a tsunami of pleasure crashed over him. His body shook as Pip stole his soul. Pip was definitely going with Savage wherever Savage went next. He would find a way to broach the topic tomorrow. Pip was his. One way or another, Pip would be his forever.

❖

PIP STROKED SAVAGE'S HAIR AND FOUGHT himself. There were so many words and too much time had passed. Savage was his mate. They had to talk about that. Not claiming Savage was making him insane with the constant unquenchable desire. The fire beneath his skin wouldn't ease until Savage claimed him. He had been thinking about it for months. Pip didn't want to take Savage's blood without his permission, and he didn't know how to get Savage to take his blood without asking.

He had been practicing his speech for a while. With Savage hovering on the edge of sleep, it seemed like a good time to dive in. "You know my family is a little different." That was probably a vast understatement, but Pip pressed on. "Anyhow, as you know, there are quite a few triad marriages in my family."

Savage peeked open one eye. "No. I don't share."

In spite of Pip's nervousness, a happy hum ran through him at Savage's possessiveness. He loved that. "That's not what I planned to say."

With a sharp nod, Savage closed his eyes. "Proceed."

Pip smiled at Savage's patient tone. "My point was their marriages are not exactly recognized by law, so in my family, we have this weird sort of tradition. A marriage ceremony of sorts." He felt dumb as hell. He knew he would eventually have to tell Savage everything, but he wasn't ready. Unfortunately, the desperation to mark Savage as his mate got worse every day. He had to do something. "Um, it's kind of like a blood oath—like becoming blood brothers... except I would taste your blood and you would taste mine." Pip said the final bit fast, hoping to get it over quick.

Silence met his words.

Pip couldn't take it. "I'd like to do that. With you," he clarified, because he was a wreck.

"No."

Pip's heart fell. "So you don't want to be my forever mate?"

Savage blew out a tired-sounding breath. His eyes didn't open. He wasn't invested at all. Pip swore he could feel how little this conversation meant to Savage. "You're in my bed, Pip. I have no plans of anyone else being here. We're good."

Damn. Pip had heard stories of mates being rejected. It was rare, but it happened. Pip never dreamed it would happen to him. He couldn't breathe. For four months, Pip had fought his nature. He had stuck to changing into his fox form in short bursts—like when he was alone in the bathroom or sometimes when Savage fell asleep. Pip had been denied the pleasure of biting his mate and taking them to new heights. There was always this piece missing. The weight of not being able to claim his mate was choking the life from Pip, and now he knew why. His mate didn't want him. Savage didn't want the permanence of a claiming. Savage only wanted to fuck him. Pip's submission fed Savage but left Pip starving.

Anger rose in Pip's chest. Celeste had known. She had to have seen this. There was no way she had been ignorant of his future. She had sent him to this heartbreak of a half life. Worse than that, it was a half life where he had to keep his fox form hidden. He didn't understand. Everyone who supposed to love him didn't. Pip was alone. Everything was pointless. He was no one's baby. Pip was just their toy.

Pip slipped from the bed. Savage was already asleep and done with dealing with Pip's needs. That was fine. Pip could be done too. He took off his collar. If Savage didn't want him forever, it was just a necklace. He shifted into fox form and called upon the small amount of power he possessed. Pip might be just a godling, but he wasn't helpless. He focused on the room he had been assigned for visits at King Jonathan's. Savage's bedroom disappeared. The air turned heavier as he shifted through space and moved farther away from his mate. Pip opened his eyes. A whine escaped him once it was done. His heart shattered. He wanted to die. The thought of never being whole again crushed him. A bright light flashed, and Celeste appeared. Pip scampered beneath the bed.

"Tell me what's wrong. I can feel you hurting."

"*You sent me away to a mate who doesn't want me. You don't get to talk to me now.*"

Celeste climbed onto the bed to look between the bed and the wall, as if trying to get a look at Pip. "What are you talking about? Savage loves you. I sent you to your happily ever after."

"*No. You just didn't want me anymore and he doesn't love me. You're supposed to be my mommy. Mommies don't hurt their babies. You sent me away.*"

Celeste tried harder to see his face. "That's not true at all, baby. I love you. It's killing me not getting to see you every day, but I want you to be happy with your soulmate. Do you honestly think I would give up your company if I didn't know in my heart that Savage is prefect for you? I was incredibly careful about who I chose for you."

Pip pressed his nose to the corner, uncaring if he was being a bratty baby. He was her baby and Celeste had sent him to his heartbreak. *"He may be perfect for me, but he doesn't want me."*

"Did he say he doesn't want you?"

Pip thumped his foot. *"Don't you know? I thought you knew everything."*

"I don't spy on you every second of the day, baby. That would be weird."

Pip hunkered down. He knew Celeste could

force him from beneath the bed. He wouldn't make it easy, though. Pip was heartbroken, upset, and done with everyone. He had done everything Savage asked. Pip had tried to be the perfect mate and it hadn't mattered. He wasn't good enough.

"Answer me, Pip. Did he say he doesn't want to be your mate?"

"*Yeah*." The single word rang through Pip's mind. It nearly broke him. He had never hurt this much.

"Oh, hell no." Celeste was gone before Pip could react.

Pip closed his eyes and focused on the raw power that always lived inside him. He drew upon its strength, hoping it would be enough to survive this. The hum didn't drown out Savage's voice in Pip's head. He could still hear Savage saying no. It had been a single-word answer with no need for explanation. Firm. Cuttingly decisive. Savage knew his mind and heart. He didn't want Pip forever. Pip was a temporary pet to Savage. Pip would never understand. How could he feel so much while Savage felt nothing? It wasn't fair. Fair had never counted when it came to him. So Pip wouldn't play anymore.

I CAN'T HURT YOU WITHOUT HURTING PIP, but I can make you wish you were dead. You will.

Savage's eyes shot open. The voice from his dream still hung in the air. He tried shaking away the ominous feeling in his gut. Savage had no reason to feel threatened. In fact, he couldn't recall ever feeling like he was in danger. He had no idea what had awoken him or brought on such a weird dream. Savage rolled. Pip was gone. Savage's gaze shot around the room. Pip's collar was on the nightstand. Savage's eye twitched. He rolled from the bed. Pip wasn't in the house. He could feel Pip missing from him. Their odd conversation from before Savage fell asleep came back to haunt him. He had felt the way he had hurt Pip when he had told him no. Savage had honestly thought Pip's reaction had to do with Savage never telling him no before. This was important, though. Savage had told him no for his own good. It also seemed ridiculous for Pip to want a strange ceremony so badly he would leave over it. If Pip had asked to get married or whatever, Savage could indulge that. It seemed Pip's request had been more important than Savage had realized.

He needed coffee if he had to face Pip's crazy-ass family to chase after Pip. Fuck. He should have listened a little harder. There had been a certain insecurity in Pip's voice. Pip had fed him too well before diving into such an important conversation. Plus, sometimes sleep took Savage without his permission when there was work to be done on the other side. Savage hadn't been thinking clearly. The more he thought about Pip being gone, the angrier he got. His anger and hurt fed his fear. Savage had nothing to lose that he cared about other than Pip. His eye twitched again. It was getting harder to hold the devil at bay. Maybe he shouldn't have been so rash with giving up the boxing career. He needed the release.

Savage plugged in the coffeemaker. A shock raged through his body, stopping his heart before restarting it. Savage gasped for air while staring at his coffeemaker. It seemed fine. There was no smoke and the clock flashed twelve. He hadn't imagined things. He had gotten fucking electrocuted. While moving a little more carefully, Savage filled it with beans and water. He pushed the button and the water began to percolate with no worries. With the coffee on, Savage went in search of clothes. By the time he dressed and brushed his teeth, the coffee was done. He grabbed a travel mug. His nerves were getting worse by the second. Savage swore he could feel Pip's pain. He picked up the coffeepot. It burst in his hand, sending glass and scalding hot water raining down his legs. Savage danced his way out of his pants while cutting his feet to ribbons. Both eyes were twitching by the time Savage cleaned up the mess and found more clothes. This time, he remembered to grab Pip's collar. Pip would not be taking it off again. Everything was shit. Savage did not like being left alone in bed. Pip was supposed to be sleeping. It was bedtime, for fuck's sake. Pip would be completely off his schedule after this shit. That was unacceptable.

Savage headed for the door. His shoes were gone. All of them. He took a breath. The air smelled sweet. He definitely wasn't alone. The bad luck since waking wasn't a coincidence. It was purposeful. Savage recalled the voice from his dream. He didn't have time for this shit. Pip was out there, hurting and alone. Savage couldn't fuck anyone up right now. He left barefoot. As he reached his truck, the lights flashed, and the doors unlocked. He grabbed the door handle and pulled. Nothing happened. He tried again, pulling even harder. The door opened with enough force, it hit him in the face, nearly knocking him on his ass.

He refused to acknowledge the benevolent spirit taunting him. Instead, Savage climbed inside his truck. He breathed a sigh of relief when it started without issue. The roll of thunder sounded throughout his truck. That was all the warning Savage got before a deluge of rain poured down on his head. Savage was beyond enraged. Still, getting to Pip was more important than the water flooding the cab of his very expensive truck. Savage seethed as it poured inside his vehicle all the way to the middle of the swamp. As he reached Pip's family's estate, the eye twitching was out of control. He was one more inconvenience away from losing control. He shoved his way from the truck. The rain cloud followed. Savage stormed the house, stopping for nothing. Not even the singular cloud that rained only for him.

Savage didn't slow to knock. He kicked open the front door, leaving it swinging from the hinges.

Jonathan looked up from his spot, lounging on the couch with his men. He glowed like the sun and dark wings pillowed him. He looked nothing like the human he had first presented himself as being. "This house has rules about knocking."

Savage showed Jonathan his true face. His voice came out sounding deep and as evil as he felt as he spoke through clenched teeth. "Death answers to no one. Not even you."

Jonathan eyed him for a moment, obviously

taking in the rain cloud and lightning that periodi-cally zapped Savage's skin. "Fair enough. I see you pissed off my grandmother. Pip is in his bedroom."

With a nod, Savage headed down the hall. His footsteps sounded like thunder as they pounded the floor and shook the ground. His temper was gone. Savage could no longer contain the power inside him. He tore open Pip's bedroom door with more force than necessary. Savage could hear Pip's heart beating beneath the bed. He dropped to his knees. Water dripped from his hair as he looked under the bed. There was a fox curled up in the corner. Savage's anger ebbed as he recognized the fox as Pip. That explained so much. He could feel the pain pulsing from Pip.

Savage settled onto his side next to the bed and stared at the fox.

Finally, Pip looked his way. "*Why are you here?*"

Savage heard the voice in his head. It was louder than Pip's usual thoughts. It wasn't background noise. Pip spoke to him in his mind. Savage wouldn't pretend he couldn't hear. "It's raining on me."

"*So?*"

Savage fought a smile. Pip was being the bratty boy tonight. "I also got electrocuted by the coffee-maker, spilled a pot of hot coffee down my legs while cutting my feet on the broken coffee pot, and then got punched in the face by my truck door."

Pip's gaze moved over Savage's face. "*You survived. Why are you here?*"

Savage rolled to his back. "It's still raining on

126

me." He relaxed into his true form. Pip wasn't hiding, so Savage wouldn't either. When his feathered top hat materialized, Savage covered his face to protect it from the rain that tried to drown him. He would stay here as long as Pip did.

He felt Pip inch closer. "*You're a Baron.*"

Savage lifted the hat and glanced Pip's way. He dipped his chin. "And you're a shifter."

"*You're not THE Baron, though*," Pip said, ignoring Savage's observation.

Savage shook his head. "I'm one of his seven sons. I'm in charge of violent deaths."

"*Oh. Okay.*"

Savage was beyond angry again. Pip always accepted everything with no questions, and he never explained himself. They couldn't move forward without talking to each other. Savage honestly didn't believe he had done anything to make Pip believe he was this fucking hard to talk to. He rolled to his side. "Do you have no questions? Why would you be so flippant about being trapped with death?"

Pip eased a little closer. "*I'm not a shifter. I'm Goddess Celeste's fur baby and a godling. This house isn't really my home. I live in the heavens with Celeste when I'm not with you. Technically, I've always been surrounded by the souls of the dead.*"

Despite his anger, a smile touched Savage's lips. "Ah. A goddess. That explains the malevolent rain cloud. I never get to meet the deities. I only sort the dead. When she came to me, I knew she wasn't human, but I couldn't decide what she was."

"*Celeste came to you?*"

"The night we met. She showed up at the pavilion after you left and suggested I not let you walk alone."

Pip eased backward, retreating. "*She set me up to fail at being a mate. You don't love me. No one does. I'll tell Celeste to leave you alone.*" He turned his back on Savage and moved back to the corner beneath the bed. Pip was obviously done talking.

Savage couldn't have that. "What do you mean she set you up to fail as a mate?"

Pip growled. "*You're my mate, but you don't want me. Therefore, I failed as a mate. It doesn't happen often, but I managed it.*"

"I'm not from your world. I don't know anything about mates. Explain."

Pip turned around and eyed Savage, as if looking for any indication that he lied. Savage stared back, refusing to hide his true self. If Pip really wanted him forever, he needed to see the evil hidden beneath human skin.

Pip became human.

Savage hoped that was a good sign.

Pip eased a little closer. "We were chosen by the goddess to be one soul. I'll always feel you missing from me, if we're not together. You'll always feel me missing from you too. Don't worry, though. I understand that you don't want me. I'll go to the heavens where emotions are muted. We never completed a blood exchange, so you'll have the freedom to go on without me. Maybe you can ask Jonathan or Tam to wipe your mind. You'll be fine."

"I'll never be fine without you, and it has nothing to do with what your goddess chooses. You are mine. You accepted your collar. I didn't realize this mating thing was so important to you, and I didn't understand why you would want to stay tied to me.

By no means did I want you to leave, though. You didn't fail. I was only looking out for you when I told you no. I'm not sure if it's safe for you to taste my blood."

Pip looked hopeful.

That hope fed Savage's confessions. "As to not loving you, that's bullshit. You're the only thing I love in this valley of endless death."

Pip blinked away tears. They dropped to the floor, sounding like a grenade to Savage's heart. "I don't know what you mean by valley of death." He reached for Savage, obviously unafraid of Savage's skeletal state. "Show me."

"I absolutely will not be doing that. It's my job to shelter you." He took Pip's hand. "I will show you what I see when I look at you, though." He let Pip see through his eyes. Everything was either on

131

fire or decaying. It was a deathscape all around them, but he stayed focused on Pip, and Pip was untouched. He was a bright beacon of beautiful life. The spot where he lay was the only place in the room untouched by death. "Everything dies, but not you. You are completely uncorrupted by me. The first time I saw you, I was ensnared. What if you taste my blood and it's the thing that kills you?"

Pip moved closer until he could cuddle up against Savage's side. "Celeste would never let that happen." The rain stopped immediately, and Savage was dry, giving power to Pip's claim. "Plus, I know you would keep me safe."

Savage was fascinated by Pip's belief in him. He had to show Pip the same trust. "Is this mate thing the reason I always have the uncontrollable urge to bite you when I'm inside you?"

Pip blushed. Savage hadn't seen him do that in a while. "Yes. You might always feel that way. I don't know, but I know that I never feel peaceful anymore because you haven't claimed me. Until you mark my skin, I'll never feel completely wanted."

Every word Pip spoke made Savage hotter by the second. His teeth itched. Savage's body shifted back to human. He found himself pinning Pip to the floor. His voice remained inhuman. "Mark your skin. Do you mean bite you?"

Pip nodded. He moved restlessly beneath Savage as if ants crawled all over his skin. Savage could feel his discomfort. It was as if Pip itched from head to toe. If Savage didn't bite him, his mind might snap. He couldn't control himself. Before Savage could stop himself, his teeth tore into Pip's shoulder.

Everything disappeared. With no recollection of how it happened, Savage found himself buried inside Pip. Pip's blood filled his mouth. Savage swallowed as he fucked Pip while trapped in the pinnacle of pleasure. Savage thought his body would fly into a million pieces and then Pip's teeth sank into Savage's chest. He hadn't known. There was no way he could have known. Nothing existed outside of them. Savage knew nothing else ever would. They were forever—literally. He had been given a soul to walk the earth with him for eternity. The power overwhelmed him as an orgasm like nothing he had ever experienced rocked him to his core. He was part of Pip and Pip was part of him. The two pieces would never separate. They were something new. Savage had always been alone. He had accepted too long ago to remember that it would always be that way. Savage had never felt bitterness toward his lot. Now he resented every second he had been denied this beauty. He was moved beyond words. When Pip had asked to be accepted as his mate forever, Savage hadn't realized what he had denied him. Now he saw. He would never forgive himself, but he would give Pip everything on a silver platter from this day on. They were something new. Something perfect. Savage was home.

PIP ACHED FROM HEAD TO TOE while also feeling like he rode the stars. As he came down from his high and Savage snapped the collar around his neck where it belonged, Pip realized he might have been a tad dramatic since leaving.

A soft and sexy chuckle rumbled from Savage as he settled down on his side next to Pip on the floor. "Celeste will understand. You're our spoiled baby boy. Plus, you're not the one she was angry with. It's me she hit with lightning bolts for a forty-five-minute drive."

A tiny part of Pip wanted to pout at being called spoiled. It was true, though. He couldn't argue. Instead, he winced. "I'm sorry about that."

Savage's gaze moved over Pip's face. "I'm not, but we do need a new coffeemaker."

"I'll make you one."

Savage's eyebrows rose. "Can you do that?"

Pip slapped his hand on the floor and a newer state-of-the-art coffee machine appeared. "Godling," he reminded Savage. "I can't do everything a god can do or even as much as a lesser god, but I have a little power."

A bright smile lit Savage's face. "Does that mean you could've handled Steve in the ring?"

A laugh burst from Pip. "I would have slaughtered him, but you did that, didn't you?"

Savage's smile slipped away. "Do I scare you?"

Pip knew what Savage really wanted to know was if he disgusted Pip. "Never." He moved closer and buried his nose against Savage's chest. "You have no idea how wild your scent drives me. It's like a campfire and the leaves on the ground in the fall." He inhaled. "You're like the sun on heated skin and the desert sands."

Savage kissed him. It was soft, but images of Pip gripping the sheets filled his head. An unsteady breath stuttered through their kiss. Savage was like flashing red lights while getting fucked just right. He was an addiction. Pip was hooked for life.

"It's time for bed, baby boy." Savage scooped Pip from the floor and carried him to bed. "We'll stay here tonight so I can apologize to Jonathan tomorrow for kicking in his front door."

A laugh caught in Pip's throat. "I'm sure it's fine. Jonathan is king of the Americas. He's also powerful enough to end several planets with the snap of his fingers. I doubt a broken front door bothers him."

Savage cuddled Pip and kissed his ear. "Still. It's the principle of the thing."

Pip understood. He needed to go to Celeste tomorrow and tell her how sorry he was too. He felt Celeste's warm touch. *"You'll always be my baby. I*

know you weren't angry. You were hurt. We are al-
ways okay."

"I love you."

Pip said the words aloud, hoping Celeste knew
they were meant for her and Savage.

Savage squeezed him against his chest. "I love
you too."

"*What he said,*" Celeste whispered against his
ear.

The night had been terrible and wonderful and
everything in between. He knew they still had
things to discuss. There had obviously been topics
they had avoided that needed to be dragged to light,
but they were one now. Nothing else mattered in
their world. They had an eternity. It was okay to rest
for now.

Chapter Six

WITH PIP GONE TO THE HEAVENS TO visit Celeste, Savage couldn't avoid venturing from the bedroom to explore the king's home any longer. The last time he had been here without Pip, Savage had been handed a kilt and told how to get to Pip's room. Now, after last night, he half expected to be escorted out. Luckily, Pip had made him some clean clothes to wear. It was a bit funny to him now how much he had been spoiling Pip with things Pip could pull from thin air. When Savage had pointed that out, Pip had looked at him with his heart in his eyes and sworn there was nothing he could do for himself that Savage couldn't do better, because Savage's gifts were laced with love. While looking into Pip's eyes, Savage believed. Now that he was alone, he hoped it was true. Otherwise, he had nothing to offer.

"You have complete acceptance to offer. There's nothing more important to a two-world being like Pip."

Savage spun to find Jonathan trailing behind him and following him from room to room. He wondered how long that had been going on. Plus, apparently, Jonathan could read his mind.

Jonathan smiled. His eyes swirled like pots of molten gold. It was mesmerizing. "I can read everyone's mind. Don't take it personally. You can't block it. That doesn't make you less powerful."

"Pip says you can snap your fingers and destroy several worlds. What do you think would happen to me if you did?"

"Let's not find out," Jonathan said, closing the

distance between them. "Let's go for a walk." Jonathan snapped his fingers and they were on the edge of a lake. He fell into step beside Jonathan as Jonathan walked along the edge. "You knew none of us were human the first time you came here."

"Yes, but I didn't know what you were," Savage answered honestly. "Everyone I see has a certain almost aura about them. It's like an hourglass in a way. When I look at people, I know exactly how much longer they'll live by the decay of their skin. Everyone is born with an assigned number of days. From there, they spoil a little more each day until death takes them. Each time I've come across immortals, I've simply stayed away. You're not my job... unless you suddenly are. I've never had a reason to learn anything about you."

"That must be a tiresome job."

"Actually, I do it quite literally in my sleep. When I wake up, I'm exhausted the way most people are when they come home from work each day. I'm not sure why, but I don't feel as tired here."

"It's me... and Tam, but don't repeat that part. We are sort of like nuclear power plants, powering everything around us. Humans can't find this place unless they're intentionally led here. This place doesn't exist on any map, but we're fun—like an amusement park in the middle of Death Valley, except we have alligators, and tigers." Jonathan seemed to think it over. "And mermen and wolves. There's also a Phoenix and sometimes we have to fight demons, but that's not the point. The point is that maybe your life doesn't have to be so isolated. I know you have Pip now, but I have this enormous estate and endless nonexistent land. I'm not asking you to fight beside us or show us favor, but maybe you don't have to be alone."

Savage tried processing all the extensive info Jonathan had dumped on him in his spiel to get to the point. "Are you asking me to live here?"

"Yes." Jonathan made a slashing motion before Savage could answer. "I know that's asking a lot, and no matter what you decide, the offer will still always be there. Here, you wouldn't have to move around and hide for fear of people discovering you're immortal. You could have as much or as little privacy as you'd like. I understand you have a very dominant personality."

A laugh rumbled in Savage's throat. Jonathan truly saw everything.

Jonathan flashed him a smile. "You'll find no

judgment here. Mates are cherished above everything in our world. The relationship between mates is a very powerful thing." Jonathan took a breath and stopped. He faced Savage. "Whatever you decide, you're a part of the family now. We'll always have your back. If you have any expensive shoes that you love, hide them. Faolan is an unrepentant shoe thief."

Savage shrugged. "Celeste already stole my shoes."

A laugh burst from Jonathan. "Damn. I don't envy your position. You'll never win a fight with Pip."

Savage stroked his chin, relishing the idea of a challenge. "I don't know. I'm pretty mean and notoriously underhanded when I want my way. I might surprise you." Savage's head automatically turned without permission from his brain. He felt Pip heading his way. A smile stretched his lips as he spotted a fox hopping and bouncing through the grass, pouncing on the gods only knew what. Savage could feel his delight with the freedom of being himself. He saw Jonathan's offer from a different angle. Pip shouldn't have to hide. He should be free to run through the grass and squish mice. In the city, he would never have this freedom. His shoulders fell when he thought about his trampoline room.

"Damn. If only I could move my house here."

"Done." Savage's house appeared at the edge of the lake, damn near knocking Savage off his feet in the impact.

"Holy shit."

Jonathan looked guilty. "Should I put it back? Do you not like it there? Does it need to move a foot to the left? I'll respect your decision if you want me to put it back. Say literally anything."

"Anything."

"Works for me." Jonathan disappeared, leaving Savage to drag his gaze between his house's new address and Pip and back again. The closer Pip flounced his way, the clearer Pip's thoughts sounded in Savage's head.

"Oh, I hear you under there, you little fucker. I'm about to pounce on your head."

A laugh burst from Savage. He had no idea what had happened to his life since meeting Pip, but he couldn't be happier. From where he stood, he could see the light twinkling on Pip's collar. Peace settled deep inside his chest. An evil smile stretched his lips. He sat and waited for Pip to burn off some energy. Soon, he would make Pip get on his knees and he needed Pip to be able to stay still. Life was perfect. He would stay. Pip would always be his. It was a flawless eternity.

Keep an eye out. Hopefully, more Hellish will be coming soon.

Please consider leaving a review at the retailer where you purchased this book. Reviews really help with a book's visibility, which allows me to continue writing more stories. Thank you, Charity.

About the Author

Charity Parkerson is an award-winning and multi-published author with several companies. Born with no filter from her brain to her mouth, she decided to take this odd quirk and insert it in her characters.

*Eight-time Readers' Favorite Award Winner
*2015 Passionate Plume Award Finalist
*2013 Reviewers' Choice Award Winner
*2012 ARRA Finalist for Favorite Paranormal Romance
*Five-time winner of The Mistress of the Darkpath

Connect with her online:

—Sign up for my newsletter: https://sendfox.com/charityparkerson
—Join my readers' group on Facebook: http://bit.ly/CharitysTribe
—Website: charityparkerson.com —
Facebook: facebook.com/authorCharityParkersonfacebook.com/TheMenofSin—Twitter: twitter.com/CharityParkerso
—Instagram:

Instagram.com/sinnerauthor
—Bookbub:
https://www.bookbub.com/authors/charity-parkerson
—Amazon page:
author.to/CharityParkerson
(http://author.to/CharityParkerson)